Raven's Secret

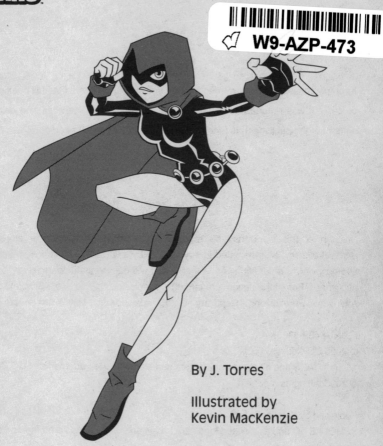

By J. Torres

Illustrated by
Kevin MacKenzie

Scholastic Inc.

New York   Toronto   London   Auckland   Sydney
Mexico City   New Delhi   Hong Kong   Buenos Aires

No part of this work may be reproduced in whole or in part, or stored in a retrieval system, or transmitted in any form or by any means, electronic, mechanical, photocopying, recording, or otherwise, without written permission of the publisher. For information regarding permission, write to Scholastic Inc., Attention: Permissions Department, 557 Broadway, New York, NY 10012.

ISBN: 0-439-69636-4
© 2005 DC Comics
TEEN TITANS and all related characters and elements are trademarks of DC Comics
© 2005. All rights reserved.

Published by Scholastic Inc.
SCHOLASTIC and associated logos are trademarks and/or registered trademarks of Scholastic Inc.

12 11 10 9 8 7 6 5 4 3 2 1   5 6 7 8 9/0

Designed by Carisa Swenson
Printed in the U.S.A.
First printing, March 2005

Chapter One

Once Upon a Crime . . .

My name is Raven. I'm called "the mysterious Teen Titan." Sometimes, "the dark and brooding one." Or even, "the creepy one." I also get "the sarcastic one" a lot.

Whatever.

I admit the dark hood and cape gives off a mysterious vibe. But just because I keep to myself doesn't mean I'm brooding. Usually, I'm just meditating. I have to. Meditating keeps me calm and centered, which prevents me from losing control over my powers. Weird things have been known to happen when I lose control of my powers.

For example, one day I went to the library to borrow a book of fairy tales. Not one of those sugar-coated kiddie collections with pointless stories about unicorns, rainbows, and pixie dust. Please. I'm talking about a classic collection of old world fairy tales about dark woods, creatures under bridges, and magic spells gone wrong.

One minute I'm coming out of the library. The next, I'm lying on the sidewalk. Turning a corner never hurt so much.

I was run over by a pale-skinned, pink-pigtailed girl dressed in purple and black named Jinx. She's one the bad guys. Jinx is bad luck. Literally.

My teammates were chasing Jinx down the

street because she had just tried to steal a Fabergé Egg from the museum. My teammates, by the way, are the Teen Titans:

Robin, who's a martial arts expert . . .

Starfire, who's an alien powerhouse . . .

Cyborg, who's a high-tech, half-teen, half-machine . . . and Beast Boy, who's green and hyper, whether he's in boy form or one of his many beast forms.

Anyway, the Titans were pursuing Jinx down the street. She turned the corner. I was coming from the other direction. I turned the corner and . . .

WHAM-O!

The world spun around me. Or I spun around the world. I couldn't really tell for sure. Nor could I tell you exactly what happened next.

My guess is that the pages of my book of fairy tales came apart when we collided. Jinx and I smashed together and somehow my supernatural powers and her hex powers caused some kind of reality-bending cosmic explosion.

The sky was now a nauseating pink color. The sidewalk was now made of cheesy, shimmering yellow brick. Those pages that flew out of my book and were now slowly floating to the ground . . . now they were blank.

They were blank because everything in them had fallen out.

Out into the real world.

Chapter Two

Witch Way

gasped in amazement. Actually, it was more of a yelp than a gasp. And I *never* yelp. But the stuff I saw . . . steel-and-glass buildings replaced by creeping vine-covered stone castles . . . frightful-looking tangled woods where a park once was . . . weirdly-colored flowers as tall as grown men instead of lampposts lining the street . . . dragon-flies as big as Cyborg flying in the sky . . . spotted snails as big as taxis . . . and was that an actual giant beanstalk reaching into a pink cloud up ahead?

I had to say it: "Raven, you're not in Kansas any-more."

Of course, I was never in Kansas to begin with but . . . never mind.

It was all a bit unsettling. I was dizzy and unsure of myself. I only half-remembered where I was or how I got there.

Let me tell you what I saw next:

A giant, angry, honking goose.

It was heading directly for me. The goose seemed . . . mad at me?

HONK! HONK! HONK!

I instinctively raised my hands in the air and prepared to . . . I wasn't sure. In the back of my mind, I knew that raising my hands would . . . result in something. I also knew that I was supposed to say . . . something. If I said whatever it was I was forgetting to say at that point, my hands would . . . no, I couldn't remember. But the goose kept on coming.

HONK! HONK! HONK!

I then did what any sane person would do who suddenly found themselves in a Grimms' fairy tale gone wrong with an angry, giant, honking goose charging at them. I ran. Ran like the wind!

As uninviting as it was, I headed for the scary-looking tangled woods. I quickly made my way over deformed roots and under knotted branches.

After I ran blind for a while, I didn't hear any more honking, so I figured it was safe to stop. Still, I decided it was a good idea to find a way to defend myself in case the goose came back. I grabbed a thin branch that jutted out of a nearby thicket.

"OW!" cried the thin branch.

Wait a minute. *"OW!" cried the thin branch?*

It wasn't a branch after all. It was the long wooden nose of a small wooden boy!

Hey, I recognize this kid, I realized.

"Plead led go ob my nobe," he said.

"Oh. I'm sorry," I said. I let go of his nose.

"Please, don't make me go back there!" whined the wooden boy. "Tell him I'm sorry, but I don't want to go back there!"

"Okay," I replied, even though I had no clue whom or what he was talking about.

"Thank you, Blue Fairy!" he cheered.

Before I could explain that I wasn't the Blue Fairy, he ran. Ran like the wind.

I chased after the wooden boy through the forest. I lost him, but it wasn't long before I came to a clearing. There, I found a pair of rather plump children. I kind of recognized them, too. They were following what appeared to be a trail of crumbs. Or were they *leaving* a trail of crumbs?

"Gretel! Look!" said the plump boy as he spotted me.

The plump girl screamed in terror.

Oh, yeah. There's an ego boost. Someone looking at you and totally freaking out.

"We did not eat your house, witch! Leave us be!" yelled the guilty-looking boy.

"It was the green one! Take him instead, witch!" protested the girl while she tried to hide the chocolate stains on her shirtfront.

Witch? *Another* case of mistaken identity. But I wasn't going to argue with them, especially after the oh-so warm reception. They ran off, too.

Yes, ran like the wind.

Witch. Fairy. Whatever. I let them go their way and I went mine.

I just wished I knew where I was going.

Chapter Three

The Land of Odd

After those close encounters of the weird kind, I had to stop and compose myself. I instinctively sat down on the ground, crossed my legs, and closed my eyes. I had a feeling that this would help. But as I sat there in silence with my eyes shut, I also had a feeling that I was forgetting something. Forgetting to do or . . . say something . . . to keep me from getting upset . . . to calm me down . . . to stay in control . . .

To get that annoying twinkling sound out of my head!

What *was* that jingly-jangly, wind chime-like noise? I was almost afraid to open my eyes. But I did anyway.

Even though she was dressed like a ballerina who fell into a vat of glitter paint, I knew that orange skin and those big green eyes anywhere — it was Starfire!

"Most noble sorceress, welcome to the Land of Odd!" said Starfire. She sounded way too happy as she peered down at me from above.

The Land of Odd. How fitting. *Sorceress*. That's debatable. But I guess it's better than being called a witch or fairy.

"Two questions, Starfire," I said. "What's going on here? And . . . what are you wearing?"

"Oh . . ." she replied, suddenly looking dejected. "You do not like my attire? Not even my sparkly, gossamer-like wings?"

Starfire turned around in the air to show me her wings, which sprayed glittery powder in the air as they flapped.

"Well," I answered, "if a disco pixie look is what you're going for . . . I'd say mission accomplished."

"Oh, thank you!" she cheered, clapping her hands. "I have never been in a fractured fairy tale before. I was not sure what to wear."

"Fractured fairy tale . . . what do you mean?" I asked. "Do you know what's happening here?"

"Well, Robin, Cyborg, Beast Boy, and I were in pursuit of Jinx," Starfire explained. "We chased her to a street corner at which time and place you were coming in the other direction. Jinx turned the corner. You turned the corner. **WHAM-O!**"

"Wham-o," I said. "That sounds very familiar."

"Your powers of good and heroic might collided with her sinister energy and misfortune," Starfire continued. "That released the contents of your book of fairy tales to create this most peculiar but curiously wonderful world!"

At least one of us was enjoying this topsy-turvy trip.

"So, now what?" I asked.

"Oh, come now, friend Raven," she said. "Even I know how this works. This is your tale. You are the heroine. You are Princess Charming."

"Princess Charming. Cute. Can't you just tell me?" I asked.

"Do you not recall how?" she replied. "You must rescue the three princes. Then use the magic spell to find your way home. Then we get the happily ever after!"

"No, really," I said. "Do you know how to make things go back to normal?"

Starfire smiled. "Naturally there is but one way," she said. "You have to get to the end of the story!"

"Of course," I said, rolling my eyes. "So, I have to rescue the princes, find my way home, and make the happily ever after. But . . . what are *you* supposed to do?"

"I will gather the loose pages of your book, bind them together, and meet you at the end of your quest!" she replied. She sounded way too proud for someone whose wings fluttered gaudily, needlessly spreading that much gold dust everywhere.

"And we can't do this together because . . . ?"

"Because each of us has a part to play in this story!" Starfire answered. "If we did not, the outcome would not be as it should."

"And your part in all of this is to play . . . my fairy godmother?"

"Why, I'd be honored!" she replied with a smile. Then she zoomed off in a streak of pink, leaving behind a whoosh of pixie dust.

Now I had a mission. I also had a good idea who the "three princes" were that I had to rescue. So, I find them, use the magic spell, and I get to go home.

I just wish I had thought to ask what that magic spell was.

Chapter Four

Great Eggspectations

Why Starfire didn't just tell me where Robin, Cyborg, and Beast Boy were, I have no idea. But I suppose that's like asking why a girl with 20/20 vision would mistake a wolf for her grandmother. Or why a seemingly bright boy would trade a perfectly good cow for a handful of beans. Or why a cow would jump over the moon. Or why anyone would jump over a candlestick.

The story simply wouldn't be the same.

Speaking of which, my story continued as I approached that giant beanstalk. There, running towards that beanstalk, was Jinx.

Under any other circumstance, I would never

consider a Jinx sighting a good thing. But I'd never been happier to see a super-villain in my life. That's not sarcasm. If Starfire was right, Jinx and I had somehow created this wacky world together, and so we had some part to play in this story that only could be resolved together. I couldn't let her get away.

As Jinx climbed the beanstalk, the leaves she stepped on turned brown and fell to the ground. Her bad-luck powers were still in full effect. I knew I had some. I just couldn't remember what they were. Or how to use them.

I should have remembered to ask Starfire.

In any case, something inside me was telling me that I should climb the beanstalk, following Jinx. I had a feeling I'd find some answers up there. But I also knew that trouble waited up in that pink cloud. Pink is a color that haunts me.

Up the beanstalk I went. I wondered what awaited me above the pink clouds. Then I remembered the giant goose.

Of course, I realized. *A giant beanstalk. A giant goose.*

If I was remembering the story correctly, there should be golden eggs and a castle up there. Plus, unfortunately, a hungry giant.

Hmm, maybe that's why Jinx is headed up there, I thought. *To steal one of the golden eggs!*

Eventually I reached the top. There was nauseatingly pink sky all around me. All I could see was pink to the left and right and above and below me. All I could hear was a disturbing, muffled voice coming from somewhere in the pink distance.

The first thing I saw was the ever-greedy Jinx carrying a giant, golden goose egg on her back. A number of other eggs were lying around on wads of pink fluff.

Wait a minute, I thought.

The fluffy pinkness I had just climbed through was not a cloud at all. There was no giant castle up here. Thankfully, no hungry giant either. Just a bunch of golden eggs sitting in a giant goose's

nest! Huh. Not exactly the way the fairy tale goes, but then again nothing around here was exactly what it should be.

Like that creepy muffled voice I heard. It shouldn't be coming from inside the giant golden egg on Jinx's back.

Chapter Five

Shell Shock

"Tell me you can throw your voice," was the first thing Jinx said to me.

"Yeah, I came all this way up a giant beanstalk to show you my new ventriloquist act," was my response to her.

The voice coming from inside the egg was hard to make out.

"Eel pirate's gold?" I repeated what I thought the egg said. Whatever that meant.

"I think it said . . . clean . . . toilet bowl?" Jinx guessed.

The egg wobbled on Jinx's back. She leaned left to keep it from rolling off. The egg shifted again.

Jinx lifted her right shoulder so she wouldn't drop it.

"Een idans d'oh!" said the voice inside the egg.

I wondered if these were magic words. Maybe even the magic words Starfire had told me about. I looked around and didn't see her. If those were the magic words Starfire had spoke of, she should have appeared by now.

"Team . . . items . . . dough?" asked Jinx as she weaved left, then right, to keep up with the quivering egg.

Team items dough? I thought. Something was coming back to me. The words rang a bell.

Team . . . items . . . dough?

No! Not dough! Go!

"Team items, go!"

"What did you say?" asked Jinx, looking annoyed.

"Er . . . that doesn't quite sound right," I replied.

Team . . . my team. The TITANS! That was it, of course!

"TEEN TITANS . . . GO!" I yelled.

They weren't magic words, but something about that . . . exclamation . . . that cheer . . . that battle cry . . . made me jump up and charge at Jinx.

I ran and leaped into a kung fu-like kick I didn't even know I knew how to do. Or maybe I knew how but had forgotten. Remember, I had been forgetting a lot of stuff.

So, I ran, leaped, and kicked, aiming for Jinx. She saw me coming and ducked just in time. My forceful flying foot connected with the giant golden egg on her back.

CRACK!

The egg began to break. It lurched off Jinx's back and landed in its fluffy pink nest. The crack I made spread in a few directions across its surface.

As bad luck would have it, the giant goose that laid that giant golden egg decided to return to its giant nest atop the giant beanstalk. And yes, as bad luck would have it, the goose saw me sail through the air and kick its golden egg. If the goose didn't have reason to be angry with me before, it did now. I fully blame Jinx for this ridiculous coincidence.

"HONK!" the goose cried. It wasn't an angry honk. It sounded more . . . *distressed*. The goose was concerned for the well-being of its egg.

The egg continued to crack. The shell broke apart, but not because of my kick or its fall. The egg was hatching now!

From inside the golden shell, a pair of green-gloved hands appeared first. Then some familiar-looking spiky black hair. Finally, a masked face I recognized right away.

"Yeah, Teen Titans, Go!" said

the hatchling. This hatchling was not a gosling. It wasn't any kind of bird. It was a boy with a bird's name.

"Robin!" I said, completely shocked to see him coming out of the giant golden egg.

Well, wouldn't you be shocked?

The giant goose certainly was. It let out another honk. But this time it was a weak and faint honk.

The goose's eyes rolled back in its head. Its neck swayed loosely in the air. Its legs trembled then gave out. The goose fell to the ground.

WHOMP!

Robin and I lost track of Jinx as we watched the woozy goose collapse.

"Did that giant goose just . . . faint?" asked Robin.

"I have to admit," I said, "I'm feeling a little shaky myself after seeing you hatch from a giant golden egg."

"Thanks for breaking me out," said Robin. "Now let's get out of here before that thing wakes up."

I turned towards the beanstalk and saw that Jinx was already on her way down.

Chapter Six

All Fall Down

"Jinx has a bit of lead," said Robin. "But if you fly us down there, we can catch her."

"*Fly? I can fly?*" I asked.

"Okay, it's more like levitating or gliding, but you know what I mean!" Robin corrected himself.

"I . . . uh . . . don't remember how to do that," I confessed.

"Just raise your hands, say the words, and off we go!" he said, rather impatiently.

"What words?" I asked.

"You know, Azarath . . . um . . . and . . ." he trailed off and began to scratch his head.

"Yes?"

"I don't remember the rest!"

"I know exactly how you feel."

Azarath. Yes, that's part of the spell, I remembered. One of the magic words in the spell Starfire told me about. Now, if I could only figure out the rest . . .

Well, just as I climbed up that beanstalk to follow Jinx, we now climbed down it after her. It was a long climb down. Robin and I had some time to compare notes.

"How did you get trapped inside a goose egg?" I asked as I jumped down off one giant leaf onto another.

"I'm not sure," replied Robin. "I only remember chasing Jinx down the street, watching her turn the corner, seeing you, and . . . **WHAM-O!**"

"Everyone remembers the wham-o part," I remarked.

"Have you seen the others?" asked Robin as he used a vine to rappel down faster.

"Only Starfire," I replied.

Robin wrinkled up his forehead like he does

when he's concerned. "Where is she now?"

"She went to bind the book that threw up this nursery rhyme nightmare," I answered. "But before she left, she said I had to get to the end of the story to get out of here."

"And how do we do that?"

"Apparently, we just have to just play our parts," I said. "I get to play Princess Charming and rescue 'three princes.' You, Cyborg, and Beast Boy are these princes."

"Well, that's one down!" he said.

Was I imagining it, or did he sound a little pleased to be called a *prince*?

I wasn't sure if I'd call what I just did a *rescue*, though. Sure, I freed Robin from his eggshell prison cell. But I didn't even know he was in there!

When Jinx reached the bottom she immediately began to cut down the beanstalk. It was like something right out of the fairy tale, but with us instead of a giant about to take a bad fall. Jinx fired waves of her purple energy blasts at the base of the over-

grown plant. Each hit shook the beanstalk hard.

"H-H-H-Hang on!" cried Robin.

"I'm t-t-t-trying!" I shouted back.

"TIM-BER!" we heard Jack — er, *Jinx* yell from somewhere beneath us.

The beanstalk tipped over like a felled tree. Robin and I held on. The beanstalk was so tall, it seemed like we fell forever and ever and ever and ever and ever and ever and ever and ever until . . .

CRASH!

The world spun around me. Or I spun around the world. Again, I couldn't really tell for sure. When I opened my eyes all I could see were strings. Each string was attached to an arm or leg of puppets dressed like cowboys.

Yee-ha.

"Did I say one down?" I heard Robin mutter from under a pile of marionettes dressed like Russian Cossack dancers. "More like two down . . . us two!"

"The question is: where did we land?" I asked, unwrapping puppet string from around my head.

Robin looked up at the hole in the roof. The leafy top of the beanstalk dangled just inside the building. He looked around the room and at all the puppets with their painted-on smiles and big, happy eyes.

"We're either in a puppet-making factory or maybe a toy store?" Robin guessed.

We both turned when we heard the sound of laughter and applause. We left the room of mangled marionettes and made our way down a darkened hall. The ropes and pulleys and the catwalk above gave us a strong clue to our location.

"We're in a theater," I said.

"And there's a show going on right now," added Robin.

We followed the sound of the audience until we got to where the curtains were gathered, and then peered out at what was happening onstage.

We couldn't believe our eyes.

Robin and I stood in the wings, gaping onstage at Cyborg . . . dancing in a chorus line!

Chapter Seven

Dancing Machine

Cyborg actually looked like he was enjoying himself. He was controlling a pair of French cancan dancer puppets with each arm. He grinned from ear to ear as he and the puppets kicked up their legs in time to the music.

"*Psst!*" called out Robin. "Cy! Over here!"

Cyborg didn't hear him.

"Dude! Over here!" Robin tried again.

"Cyborg!" I shouted.

He still couldn't hear us over the noise of the laughing, clapping crowd, the cancan music, and his own shouts of "Hey! Hey! Hey!"

Frustrated, Robin untied the rope holding the curtains back. The curtains swung closed. Cyborg stopped kicking and immediately looked over in our direction.

"Robbie! Ray!" he happily exclaimed. "Come here and meet my new friends!"

Robin and I exchanged looks of confusion and slowly inched towards Cyborg and his *new friends.*

"This is Marie and Sophie," he said, looking at the puppets on his right. "And over here is Babette and Claudette," he continued, naming the puppets on his left.

"Cyborg . . . " I said. "You do realize that your new friends are inanimate objects, right?"

"Aw, come on, Raven!" Cyborg replied. "You'll upset them if you keep talking like that."

Robin and I exchanged looks again. The audience on the other side of the curtain was getting restless. They were chanting: "Dan-cing Machine! Dan-cing Machine! Dan-cing Machine!"

"What's going on here, Cyborg?" asked Robin.

"Can't you see? I'm putting on a one-man-puppet-show-slash-dance spectacular!" replied Cyborg.

"We need to go find Beast Boy," I told him.

"Dude, I can't," said Cyborg. "I made a promise!"

"What kind of promise?" I asked.

"To do three shows a day, six days a week until the little wooden boy returns," Cyborg said. "He was the star of the show!"

"So, he promised to come back?" I asked.

"Yep, and until then I'm the whole show!" said Cyborg proudly.

"Was his nose particularly long when he made

this promise?" I then asked.

"Now that you mention it . . . his nose did seem to grow as he spoke."

"Does the name *Pinocchio* mean anything to you?" I inquired. "The long nose meant he was telling you a lie. He's not coming back."

"Then stick-boy also lied about something bad happening if I did leave," Cyborg added.

"Starfire said we all had parts to play in this story, but I doubt this is what she meant," I continued.

"Yeah," grunted Cyborg. "I should have known better than to trust someone in showbiz!"

He said his good-byes to the French puppets flopped out on the stage floor: "*Au revoir,* Marie, Sophie, Babette, and Claudette!"

"How did you end up here, anyway?" I asked Cyborg as we made our way offstage.

"I'm not sure," he replied. "I remember chasing Jinx down the street, watching her turn the corner, seeing you, and then — **WHAM-O!** — I'm playing the part of a puppeteer!"

The Land of Odd, indeed.

Chapter Eight

When Puppets Attack

Robin, Cyborg, and I quickly made our way backstage. We figured we had to get out of there before the audience rushed the stage. Little did we know that the audience was the least of our worries. We were only a few feet from the back door when . . .

"Where do you think you're going?" asked a small voice.

"Uh . . . who said that?" I asked.

Cautiously, we turned around. Slowly, out of the darkness, puppet after puppet stepped out, dragging their strings and controllers behind them. Their painted-on smiles were turned into grimaces and their big happy eyes squinted in anger.

"*Nyet!* You cannot go," insisted a Cossack dancer in a very creepy tone.

"You're the star of the show, buckaroo," said a cowboy in an equally scary voice.

"I'm sorry, guys," explained Cyborg. "I have go with my friends here."

"But *we* are your friends, *non?*" said Marie the cancan dancer. She emerged from the shadows with a sinister expression on her face.

This could only lead to one thing: a full-on zombie puppet attack.

They charged at us! Cowboys lassoed us with their strings from the left! Cancan dancers kicked us from the right! We were surrounded!

Robin pulled out some of his exploding discs.

"No, Robin! Stop!" yelled Cyborg.

Robin was baffled by Cyborg's demand.

"Raven, throw up a protective bubble between us," pleaded Cyborg. "They *were* my friends. I don't know what's come over them, but I don't want them harmed."

"A bubble?" I asked. "How do I do that?"

"Come on!" cried Cyborg. "You do it all the time! Just raise your hands, say the words, and make it happen!"

"Uh . . . could you refresh my memory?" I asked. "What words?"

"You know . . . something-something, Metrion . . . um . . . " tried Cyborg. "Something . . . Metrion and . . . " He trailed off.

"Yes?"

"I can't remember!"

"Robin and I know exactly how you feel."

Azarath. Metrion. Yes, something inside of me knew that there was only one more magic word missing to complete the spell. But for now, we only had one option.

"Run! Run like the wind," I yelled.

We ran as fast and as far away from those angry puppets as possible. Luckily, their little legs couldn't keep up with us.

"I don't get it!" said Cyborg. "How did those

puppets move on their own?"

"Why is the sky pink?" I shot back. "Why are the geese so big? How did Starfire get so sparkly? It's the Land of Odd. I stopped asking questions long ago."

"But I have a question," said Robin. "Now what?"

I didn't have an immediate answer, but I knew where to start looking for one — Jinx. She led me to Robin. She led Robin and me to Cyborg. I was picking up a pattern.

If we find Jinx, Beast Boy will most likely be close by, I thought.

"Hey . . . isn't that Jinx over there?" pointed out Cyborg at that very moment.

Chapter Nine

Into the Woods

"Teen Titans, Go!" I yelled.

We hurried after Jinx as she disappeared into a field of tall grass. We followed her and soon found ourselves ankle deep in . . . molasses? Upon closer inspection, we realized that the tall grass was actually made of licorice. Rocks on the ground were actually chunks of peanut brittle. The sticky swamp slowed us down . . .

"We've lost her," I said.

"No . . . listen!" said Robin.

We heard a sloshing sound. Then the snap of what might have been peanut brittle. Someone was on the move. We all pricked up our ears and listened carefully.

44

"That way," I whispered.

I led the boys towards some tall grass that I thought I saw moving. We approached as quietly as we could. I slowly parted the licorice whips, believing I'd find Jinx hiding behind there.

"Yo, Beast Boy!" shouted Cyborg, upon spotting a green frog.

The frog, which was sitting on a rock made of marzipan, only blinked its eyes.

"Are you sure that's Beast Boy?" I asked.

"Of course I'm sure!" insisted Cyborg. "You think I don't recognize my own best pal?"

"Then what's he doing just sitting there?" I inquired.

"Hmm," said Robin, rubbing his chin. "Didn't you say you had to rescue three princes, Raven?"

"Uh-huh," I said, wondering what Robin was getting at.

"Okay, so my being trapped in a big goose egg and Cyborg being stuck in that show weren't exactly traditional fairy-tale scenarios," he continued.

"Uh-huh," I said, not liking where this was going.

"But the frog prince thing is as classic as it gets!" exclaimed Cyborg.

"So?" I asked, even though I knew what they were going to say next.

"Come on, Raven, you know what you have to do here," said Robin.

"You have to kiss the frog to break the spell!" they said together.

I crossed my arms at that point. I did my best "dark" and "brooding" for effect. I hated to admit it, but they might have been right. But it was pointless for them to be enjoying this moment so much.

"Fine!" I said. "Just so we can get all of this over with already . . ."

I reluctantly leaned in and kissed the frog.

Nothing happened.

"Huh," said Cyborg. "Nothing happened."

"Why don't you try it again?" suggested Robin.

Both of them took a step back when I turned

and faced them. Maybe it was the glare. Maybe they even saw steam coming out of my ears. Either way, they knew I wasn't going to kiss the frog twice. Anyone who suggested it was going to get hurt.

But then . . .

From somewhere nearby we heard a moaning sound. It sounded almost ghostlike and eerie. Yet it also sounded . . . kind of familiar.

"Is it just me or does *that* sound like Beast Boy?" asked Robin.

We took a second look at the frog. The moaning was coming from elsewhere.

"Oh, yeah," said Cyborg, "that's B.B. all right."

"He sounds just like he did the time you two had that pizza eating contest," I added.

Beast Boy lost that challenge. He got sick. His stomach ached so much that he wailed like a banshee all night. We followed the familiar sound until . . .

"Yo, Beast Boy!" shouted Cyborg joyfully.

This time it really was him. Beast Boy lay on the ground, jellybeans in one limp hand, chocolate chunks in the other. His stomach was totally bloated. Behind him was a gingerbread house with a candy cane fence and a garden of lollipops like something out of the story of *Hansel and Gretel*. Except that everything was half-eaten. Which would explain Beast Boy's condition.

"So, while Robin was trapped in an egg, Starfire was playing fairy godmother, and I was chasing Jinx all over the place . . . you were here *eating*?" I asked him angrily.

"Yeah, so?" Beast Boy shot back, looking a little guilty. "What was Cyborg doing that was so important?"

"I was delighting millions with my dancing ability," Cyborg said proudly.

"You were *what?*" asked Beast Boy, now confused.

"Long story, tell you later," replied Cyborg.

I was getting cavities just looking at that gingerbread house. So I reminded Beast Boy that in the fairy tale the house belonged to a wicked witch. And that she was plenty mad at the kids who ate her home. And since those kids weren't around, he was going to get all the blame. Needless to say, he hurried us out of there.

Getting out of that forest was easy enough. We simply followed a trail of crumbs that someone cleverly had left behind. It was no mystery who left the trail. I was just surprised that Beast Boy hadn't eaten the crumbs.

"So, how did you end up at the gingerbread house?" I asked Beast Boy.

"I don't know," he replied. "I only remember chasing Jinx down the street, watching her turn the corner, seeing you, and then — **WHAM-O!** — I'm standing in front of a gingerbread house playing the part of Hansel and Gretel! How cool is it that I got to eat for two?"

"Not as cool as that," I said.

I was pointing at a gleaming tower in the distance.

Chapter Ten

Happily Never After

The tower wasn't shaped like a T like our headquarters and home, Titans Tower. It was just one tall column of gilded brick. It wasn't situated on an island like Titans Tower. It was at the top of a hill.

Yet . . . it felt like home.

It looked like one of those fabled towers where princesses are imprisoned to do impossible tasks. Like spin straw into gold. Or guess the names of total strangers. Or pretend to be sleeping until some knight in shining armor rescued them with a kiss . . .

I was jarred out of my fairy-tale thoughts by Cyborg yelling, "It's Jinx!"

She was running down the far side of that

hill. She had a mischievous grin on her face and obviously was up to no good again.

"Let's get her!" Robin shouted.

"No," I said. "Let's just get to that tower. Let's just go home."

Starfire said she'd be waiting for me with the book at the end of the quest. My quest involved rescuing three princes. I did that. She then said to use the "magic spell" to get home. This felt like home. So, I thought that all I needed to do was say the words. I had two of the three words thanks to Robin and Cyborg. Now I knew to turn to Beast Boy to complete the spell:

"Beast Boy, give me the magic word."

"Abracadabra?" he said, unsure of what I wanted.

"Not that one," I said.

"Hocus-pocus?" he asked.

"No," I said. "The one that comes after Azarath, Metrion . . . "

"Zinthos!" he shouted.

"Yes!" I said.

At that very moment, an impossibly long braid of brown hair tumbled out of the tower window. It was so long that it almost touched the ground. The boys looked at each other in disbelief.

"I guess . . . we're supposed to climb it," I said.

So climb it we did. Except for Beast Boy, who chose to transform into a nightingale and fly to the window instead. Sure enough, when we reached the window, we discovered that the impossibly long braid of brown hair was attached to Starfire. Gone was the disco pixie

outfit. She was now dressed like Rapunzel.

"Princess Charming!" she cried, way too gleefully.

She was holding my book of fairy tales with all the loose pages sandwiched between the covers.

"Okay, we're all here," I said. "This is the end of the story, right? How do we get everything back to normal?"

Then Starfire said something that I should have known she was going to say:

"Why, Raven, you've known how to do that all along."

She was right. My powers accidentally combined with Jinx's to create this loony universe. Since that big bang, it's been a tug of war between good and bad luck. But I'd been following my instincts throughout this whole misadventure. Even when things didn't make sense, I went with my gut feelings. So, I decided to keep on doing that.

I grabbed the book from Starfire and ran for the window. I leaped out and gently floated to the ground. Yes, I suddenly remembered how to levitate.

When I reached the ground, I sat with my legs crossed and placed the book in front of me. Then I closed my eyes and began to chant.

"*Azarath. Metrion. Zinthos.*"

Call it a spell, chant, or charm (Princess Charming, get it?), but it's really more than that. Those words are my mantra — words I live by. What they mean doesn't really matter (okay, that's my secret — don't pry). All that matters is that those words calm me, keep me centered. When I'm calm and centered, I keep my emotions in check. Keeping my emotions in check prevents me from losing control of my powers. And that's important because weird things have been known to happen when I lose control of my powers.

Azarath. Metrion. Zinthos.

I raised my hands in the air and ebony waves of energy burst forth. The waves swirled above me until they spun into a vortex. This funnel-shaped mass grew bigger and bigger until it swallowed me up. Before long, it looked like I was floating cross-legged in the center of a black tornado whose tail disappeared into the book on the ground.

Azarath. Metrion. Zinthos.

The black tornado twisted and whipped about, not going anywhere, but sucking in everything around it. It looked like the Land of Odd was melting and going down a dark drain . . .

There went the dragonflies as big as Cyborg! There went the giant beanstalk! There went the twisted trees from the tangled wood! There went the gingerbread house! There went the frog we thought was Beast Boy! There went the angry puppets! And there went . . . Jinx into my reality-adjusting twister!

The whole world spun around me. Or I spun around the world. I couldn't really tell for sure, but I remained calm and kept chanting . . .

Azarath. Metrion. Zinthos. Azarath. Metrion. Zinthos. Azarath. Metrion. Zinthos.

When I finally opened my eyes, I found myself lying on the sidewalk, my head spinning, pages

from my book falling out of the sky . . .

"Raven! Are you all right?" asked Starfire as she helped me sit up.

I peered around . . . the sky was blue, not a nauseating pink color . . . the sidewalk was hard and gray concrete, not cheesy shimmering yellow brick . . . and those pages that flew out of my book were not blank at all but full of words and pictures telling stories about petrified forests, trolls under bridges, and magic spells gone wrong.

"What happened?" I asked, still a little woozy.

"Well," Starfire began, "Robin, Cyborg, Beast Boy, and I were in pursuit of Jinx . . . we chased her to this street corner at which time and place you were coming in the other direction . . . Jinx turned the corner . . . you turned the corner . . . and . . . **WHAM-O!**"

"Yes, I remember the wham-o part," I said.

I also remembered a lot of other things. But seeing Robin not trapped in a giant golden goose egg . . . and Beast Boy not bloated from eating half of a life-sized gingerbread house . . . and the only dancing Cyborg was doing was his victory dance because they had captured Jinx . . . I decided to keep those Mother Goose memories to myself.

Besides, the more secrets I kept, the more dark and mysterious I seemed to be.

TITANS EAST ACTION FIGURES.
KICKING EVIL WHERE IT COUNTS.

WATCH TEEN TITANS ON
CARTOON NETWORK